ALBERT EINSTEIN

INGENIOUS PHYSICIST AND FATHER OF RELATIVITY

ALEXANDRA
HANSON-HARDING

Britannica®
Educational Publishing

IN ASSOCIATION WITH

ROSEN
EDUCATIONAL SERVICES

Published in 2016 by Britannica Educational Publishing (a trademark of Encyclopædia Britannica, Inc.) in association with The Rosen Publishing Group, Inc.

29 East 21st Street, New York, NY 10010

Distributed exclusively by Rosen Publishing.

To see additional Britannica Educational Publishing titles, go to rosenpublishing.com.

First Edition

Britannica Educational Publishing
J.E. Luebering: Director, Core Reference Group
Mary Rose McCudden: Editor, Britannica Student Encyclopedia

Rosen Publishing
Heather Moore Niver: Editor
Nelson Sá: Art Director
Nicole Russo: Designer
Cindy Reiman: Photography Manager
Bruce Donnola: Photo Researcher

Library of Congress Cataloging-in-Publication Data

Hanson-Harding, Alexandra, author.
 Albert Einstein : ingenious physicist and father of relativity / Alexandra Hanson-Harding. — First edition.
    pages cm -- (Britannica beginner bios)
 Includes bibliographical references and index.
 Audience: 1-4.
 ISBN 978-1-68048-255-3 (library bound) — ISBN 978-1-5081-0060-7 (pbk.) — ISBN 978-1-68048-313-0 (6-pack)
 1. Einstein, Albert, 1879-1955--Juvenile literature. 2. Physicists—Biography—Juvenile literature. I. Title. II. Series: Britannica beginner bios.
 QC16.E5H36 2016
 530.092—dc23
 [B]

2015018791

Manufactured in the United States of America.

CONTENTS

CHAPTER ONE

A GREAT MIND

Albert Einstein sits on a train in Germany in the early 1930s.

Albert Einstein was one of the greatest physicists in history. Physicists are scientists who study matter, which makes up all physical objects. They study the forces (pushes and pulls) that act on matter. Einstein's ideas led to new ways of thinking about the universe.

Einstein was born in Ulm, Germany, in 1879, to a loving Jewish family. From his early childhood onward, it was clear that Einstein learned in a special way. His dreamy, stubborn personality did not fit with the strict German culture of the time. His need to do things his own way often got him in trouble.

Einstein's birthplace in Ulm, Germany

However, his unique mind produced thoughts that changed the world. In one year, he wrote four papers that changed physics forever. He won a Nobel Prize, the

Einstein won the Nobel Prize for Physics in 1921.

highest honor a scientist can receive, before he was thirty years old.

Einstein experienced much turmoil throughout his life, but he continued to explore new ideas in physics until his death. Scientists still use his work to make new discoveries today.

Quick Fact

Albert Einstein's THEORIES about physics led to new ways of thinking about the universe.

Vocabulary Box

THEORIES are explanations for why things work or how things happen.

CHAPTER TWO

EARLY LIFE

When Albert Einstein was still a baby, his family moved from Ulm to the bigger city of Munich. There, his father, Hermann, ran a factory that made electrical equipment. His mother, Pauline, ran the home. She passed on her love of music to Albert, and he played the violin throughout his life. He had a little sister named Maja, who was his lifelong friend.

Einstein and his little sister, Maja, in the 1880s

Quick Fact

At age five, young Albert was fascinated by the invisible forces that move the needle of a compass.

Einstein took an early interest in the forces that act on matter.

Young Albert did well at school, often earning top marks in his classes. However, he hated his strict school when he was older. His severe teachers did not appreciate Albert's creative learning style. One teacher said he would never amount to anything.

When Albert was fifteen, his father's factory failed. The family moved to Italy, but Albert stayed behind in Germany to finish school. Six months later, Albert left Germany because he could not stand to stay at his school.

Albert fled to his parents in Italy. He spent a few months in Italy and then moved to Switzerland to finish high school. He began college courses in Zurich, Switzerland, in 1896. He also gave up his German citizenship that year.

In Zurich, Einstein studied to be a teacher. He also met a fellow physics student, Mileva Maric. They fell in love. They wanted to get married after he graduated in 1900, but it took him a long time to find a job. Einstein studied advanced subjects on

German-speaking European college students at a fencing match around the time Einstein went to college.

his own, so he often cut classes. That made some professors mad. They did not recommend him when he applied for jobs after graduation.

Einstein and his first wife, Mileva

Vocabulary Box

A **PATENT** is an official document that gives inventors control over who may use their invention.

It was not until 1902 that Einstein was able to get an acceptable job. He became a clerk in the **PATENT** office in Bern, Switzerland. Einstein married Mileva in 1903. Their children, Hans Albert and Eduard, were born in 1904 and 1910.

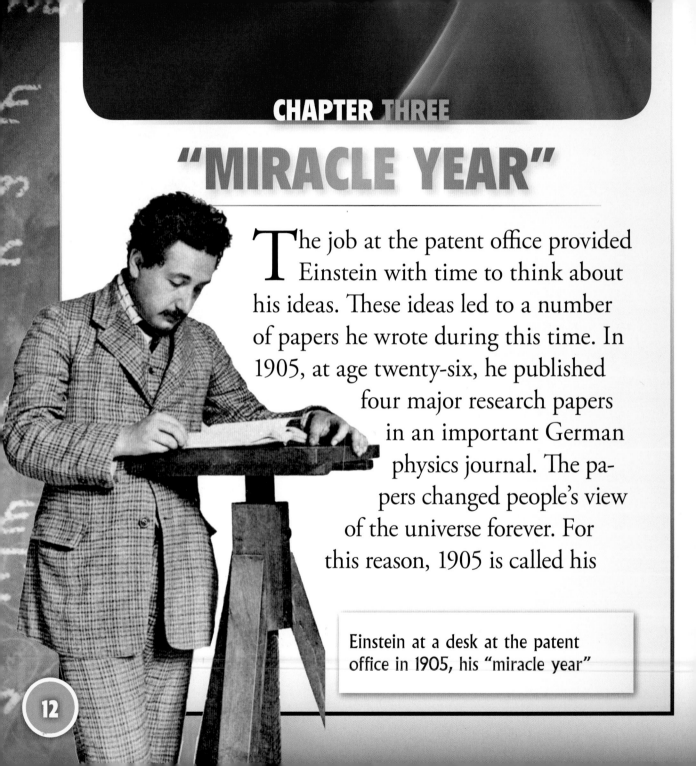

CHAPTER THREE

"MIRACLE YEAR"

The job at the patent office provided Einstein with time to think about his ideas. These ideas led to a number of papers he wrote during this time. In 1905, at age twenty-six, he published four major research papers in an important German physics journal. The papers changed people's view of the universe forever. For this reason, 1905 is called his

Einstein at a desk at the patent office in 1905, his "miracle year"

Quick Fact

Einstein did not need equipment to work out his ideas. He did "thought experiments" in his head. In one thought experiment he imagined traveling next to a light beam.

"miracle year."

One paper was about the nature of light. Scientists already knew that light is a form of energy. They also knew it behaved like waves. Einstein

Einstein showed that light is made up of particles called photons.

showed that light also behaves like particles. He said that light is made up of separate packets of energy, called photons or quanta. (A single light particle, or photon, has one quantum of energy.) This idea helped to form the radical new branch of physics called quantum physics. Quantum physics explores the tiniest bits of the universe and how they behave.

Another of the four papers helped prove that atoms were real. The tiny particles called atoms are the basic building blocks of all matter. Scientists had known about atoms for hundreds of years, but Einstein

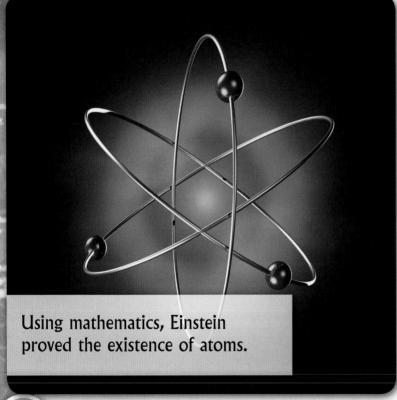

Using mathematics, Einstein proved the existence of atoms.

> ## Quick Fact
> **The speed of light is about 186,282 miles per second.**

used mathematics to prove that they existed. Einstein studied the movement of tiny particles made up of atoms. He was able to figure out the size of the atoms based on the way the particles moved about in water.

His third paper was about his "special theory of relativity." This theory states that measurements of space and time are relative. That is, they change when taken by people moving at different speeds. This idea was entirely new. The special theory of relativity also changed how scientists thought about energy and matter.

His fourth paper was also about relativity. This paper was about the relationship of mass and energy. Mass is the measure of how much matter is in physical things made of molecules, such as water or rocks or gas. Einstein wrote the world's most famous math equation

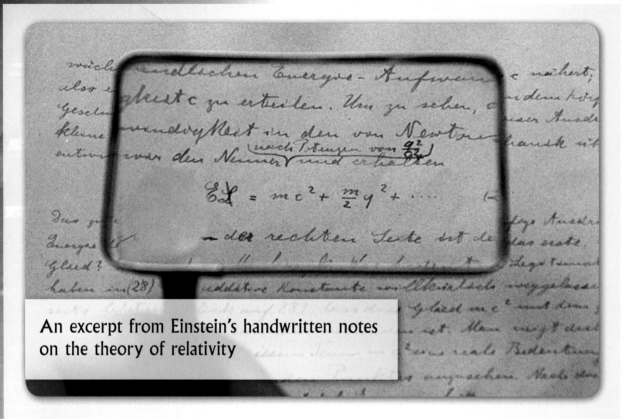

An excerpt from Einstein's handwritten notes on the theory of relativity

about it: $E=mc^2$. The equation means that Energy *(E)* equals mass *(m)* times the speed of light squared *(c²)*. It means that energy can turn into mass and mass can turn into energy. They are the same thing in different forms. The equation also shows that a tiny amount of mass is equal to a huge amount of energy.

CHAPTER FOUR

FAME

Einstein's papers were published in the *Annals of Physics*, one of the most famous physics journals in Europe. Scientists were amazed by his ideas. The papers received a lot of attention.

Einstein was offered a professorship. He rose

Über die spezielle und die allgemeine Relativitätstheorie

(Gemeinverständlich)

Von

A. EINSTEIN

Mit 3 Figuren

Braunschweig
Druck und Verlag von Friedr. Vieweg & Sohn
1917

The title page to a 1917 edition of Einstein's *On the Special and General Theory of Relativity,* hand-inscribed by the physicist himself

17

quickly in the academic world. In 1914, he accepted a job at the University of Berlin. It was one of the most respected schools in Europe for physics.

That same year, Germany entered World War I. Einstein was a pacifist, which meant he was against using violence to settle problems. Einstein often spoke out against war. He wrote, "At such a time as this, one realizes what a sorry species of animal one belongs to."

During this time he kept trying to fix his theory of special

Einstein realized that time moves more slowly near large planets, like Jupiter.

relativity. It seemed too limited to him. It only worked in a world where movement did not accelerate. If a car was moving at 20 miles (about 32 kilometers) per hour, it had to keep moving at exactly that speed for his theory to work.

Einstein also realized he needed to add **GRAVITY** to his theory. Gravity is a pulling force that works across space. According to his theory, matter pulls space and time toward it. For example, he found that time actually moves more slowly near large planets.

Vocabulary Box

GRAVITY is what gives weight to objects on Earth. Scales measure the pull of gravity as weight.

Einstein completed what he called his theory of general relativity in 1915. But it was not until 1919 that other scientists could do tests that showed that his theory was right. After the positive results were officially announced, Einstein became world famous.

Einstein and his second wife, Elsa

Also in 1919, Einstein and Mileva divorced. Later that year he married his cousin Elsa Löwenthal.

In 1921, Einstein went on a speaking tour. He visited the United States, England, Japan, and France.

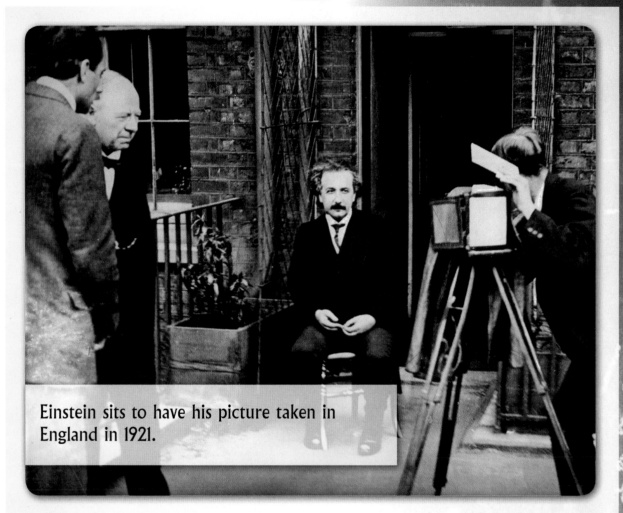

Einstein sits to have his picture taken in England in 1921.

Everywhere he went, thousands of people gathered to hear him. In 1921, Einstein was awarded the Nobel Prize for Physics.

CHAPTER FIVE

EINSTEIN IN AMERICA

I n the early 1930s, the Nazi Party was taking over Germany. The Nazis hated the Jewish people. Albert

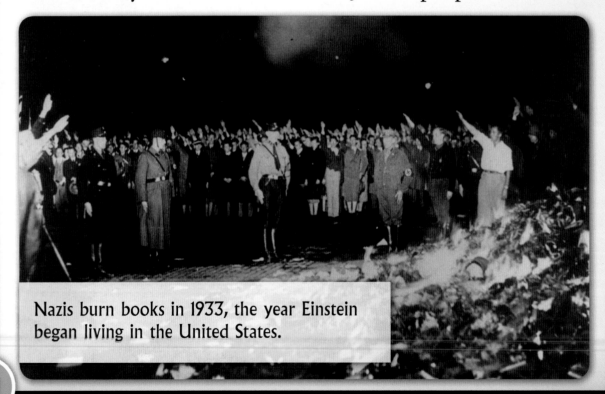

Nazis burn books in 1933, the year Einstein began living in the United States.

Einstein, one of the most famous Jewish people in the world, became a target. The Nazis burned his books. They called his work a lie. In 1931, they published a book called *One Hundred Authors Against Einstein*. They threatened his life.

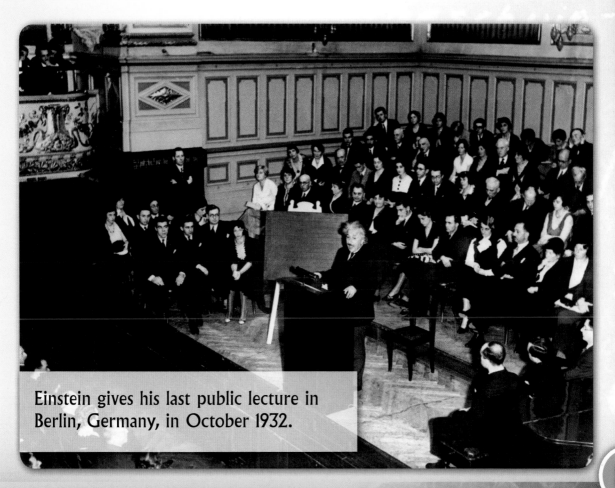

Einstein gives his last public lecture in Berlin, Germany, in October 1932.

```
                          Albert Einstein
                          Old Grove Rd.
                          Nassau Point
                          Peconic, Long Island

                          August 2nd, 1939

F.D. Roosevelt,
President of the United States,
White House
Washington, D.C.

Sir:

     Some recent work by E.Fermi and L. Szilard, which has been com-
municated to me in manuscript, leads me to expect that the element uran-
ium may be turned into a new and important source of energy in the im-
mediate future. Certain aspects of the situation which has arisen seem
to call for watchfulness and, if necessary, quick action on the part
of the Administration. I believe therefore that it is my duty to bring
to your attention the following facts and recommendations:

     In the course of the last four months it has been made probable -
through the work of Joliot in France as well as Fermi and Szilard in
America - that it may become possible to set up a nuclear chain reaction
in a large mass of uranium,by which vast amounts of power and large quant-
ities of new radium-like elements would be generated. Now it appears
almost certain that this could be achieved in the immediate future.

     This new phenomenon would also lead to the construction of bombs,
and it is conceivable - though much less certain - that extremely power-
ful bombs of a new type may thus be constructed. A single bomb of this
type, carried by boat and exploded in a port, might very well destroy
the whole port together with some of the surrounding territory. However,
such bombs might very well prove to be too heavy for transportation by
air.
```

Einstein wrote to President Franklin Roosevelt, warning that Germany could build an atomic bomb.

In 1932, Einstein left Germany. He never returned. In 1933, he settled in Princeton, New Jersey, where he joined the Institute for Advanced Study. Einstein became an American citizen in 1940.

During the 1930s, scientists began studying how energy could be released from atoms. Their studies were based on Einsten's famous equation, $E = mc^2$. The scientists began to work on a powerful new weapon that worked by releasing the energy stored in certain types of atoms. The weapon was called the atomic bomb. Einstein thought the Nazis were so dangerous that the United States should build an atomic bomb before the

Quick Fact

Einstein was offered the chance to be Israel's president. He declined.

Hiroshima, Japan, was devastated after the United States dropped an atomic bomb on it.

Nazis did. He wrote to U.S. president Franklin D. Roosevelt in August 1939 and told him so.

In 1941, the United States entered World War II. By then, many scientists in the United States were working on building the first atomic bomb. Einstein was not invited. The government did not trust him because of his pacifist past.

Vocabulary Box

The struggle for equal rights for African Americans, especially in the 1950s and 1960s, is known as the CIVIL RIGHTS MOVEMENT.

The United States dropped the first atomic bomb on Japan in 1945. After Einstein learned about the horrible damage it caused, he changed his mind again. He helped form the Emergency Committee of Atomic Scientists. This group fought the spread of atomic weapons. Einstein also fought for other causes, such as world peace and the CIVIL RIGHTS MOVEMENT.

Einstein enjoyed life around Princeton. He took walks. He talked with friends about politics, religion, and physics. Einstein also discussed his search for what he called a unified field theory. He had started working on the idea in 1925. He hoped to explain how all of the forces of the universe fit together. When he died in 1955, his theory was still unfinished.

Einstein sticks out his tongue at photographers on his 72nd birthday.

Einstein's work continues to inspire scientists. Physicists are still working on his "theory of everything."

TIMELINE

1879: Albert Einstein is born in Ulm, Germany, on March 14.

1881: Albert's sister Maria (who goes by the name of Maja) is born.

1894: Einstein's family moves to Italy, leaving him in Germany to finish school. Later that year, he joins his parents in Italy.

1896–1900: Einstein goes to college at the Zurich Polytechnic Institute.

1901: Einstein becomes a Swiss citizen.

1902: Einstein gets a job at the Swiss Patent office in Bern, Switzerland.

1903: Einstein marries Mileva Maric.

1904: The Einsteins' first son, Hans Albert, is born.

1905: During Einstein's "miracle year," at only 26 years of age, he publishes four major papers in the journal known as the Annals of Physics.

1909: Einstein becomes associate professor at the University of Zurich.

1910: The Einsteins' second son, Eduard, is born.

1911: The Einsteins move to Prague when he gets a teaching job there.

1912: Einstein accepts a job at Zurich Polytechnic Institute.

1913: Einstein accepts a professorship at the University of Berlin in Germany.

1915: Einstein completes his theory of general relativity and presents it at the Prussian Academy of Sciences.

1919: The Royal Society announces that Einstein's theory of general relativity has been proved; Einstein divorces Mileva and marries his cousin Elsa.

1921: Einstein wins the Nobel Prize for Physics.

1931: The Nazi Party attacks Einstein and his ideas.

1933: Einstein moves to Princeton, New Jersey, after Hitler comes to power in Germany.

1936: Elsa Einstein dies.

Late 1930s: European scientists use Einstein's ideas to begin to develop an atomic bomb.

1939: Einstein urges President Roosevelt to build an atomic bomb.

1940: Einstein becomes a U.S. citizen.

1945: The United States drops the first atomic bomb on Japan. Einstein starts to work against the spread of atomic bombs.

1952: Einstein turns down the offer to be president of Israel.

1955: Einstein dies on April 18.

GLOSSARY

ACCELERATE To move faster or speed up.

ATOM The smallest possible unit of an element.

CRITIC A person who judges the value of something.

ENERGY The ability to use power or to be active; to have the capacity to do work.

EQUATION A statement of the equality of two mathematical expressions.

FORCE A push or a pull acting upon an object.

MASS The amount of matter in an object.

MATTER Anything that takes up space. Air, water, rocks, and people are examples of matter.

NAZI PARTY A political group that ruled Germany between 1933 and 1945.

PHYSICS The scientific field that studies matter and the forces that affect it.

QUANTUM A specific amount of energy. The plural of quantum is quanta.

RELATIVITY A theory in physics that considers mass and energy to be equal. The theory states that a moving object will experience changes in mass, size, and time that are related to its speed and are not noticeable except at speeds approaching that of light.

BOOKS

Berne, Jennifer. *On a Beam of Light: A Story of Albert Einstein.* San Francisco, CA: Chronicle Books, 2013.

Colson, Mary. *Albert Einstein and Sir Arthur Eddington* (Dynamic Duos of Science). New York, NY: Gareth Stevens, 2014.

Delano, Marfe Ferguson. *Genius: A Photobiography of Albert Einstein.* Washington, DC: National Geographic Society, 2015

Krull, Kathleen. *Albert Einstein* (Giants of Science). New York, NY: Puffin Books, 2015.

Norwich, Grace. *I Am Albert Einstein.* New York, NY: Scholastic, 2012.

Pohlen, Jerome. *Albert Einstein and Relativity for Kids: His Life and Ideas with 21 Activities and Thought Experiments* (For Kids). Chicago, IL: ChicagoReview Press, 2012.

WEBSITES

Because of the changing nature of Internet links, Rosen Publishing has developed an online list of websites related to the subject of this book. This site is updated regularly. Please use this link to access this list:

http://www.rosenlinks.com/BBB/Ein

INDEX